Find more tales about Captain Dan
and other great all-ages books at
MonkeyMinionPress.com!

First Edition

No portion of this publication may be reproduced (except for review purposes) by any means without express written permission from Monkey Minion Press or an agent of Monkey Minion Press.

ISBN-13: 978-0615608617

ISBN-10: 0615608612

In every sailor's club at every port, would-be seamen lean close to hear stories of Captain Dan and the Grumbling Grog. Known far and wide as the fiercest pirate to ever set sail, the captain commands a crew of the scurviest scalawags ever collected on a single ship. Wizened sailors whisper quiet warnings to greener shipmates, "If you should ever see the flag of Captain Dan behind you, surrender all your treasure at once!"

Brash deckhands will scoff and swagger away, but wiser sailors nod sagely in agreement. "Never fight Captain Dan! Throw yourself on his mercy, for though he has none, he may be bored enough to let you live!"

Captain Dan and the crew of the Grumbling Grog had enjoyed a long day of harassing sailors and stealing treasure. Night had come to Bathtub Bay and with it, dinner time.

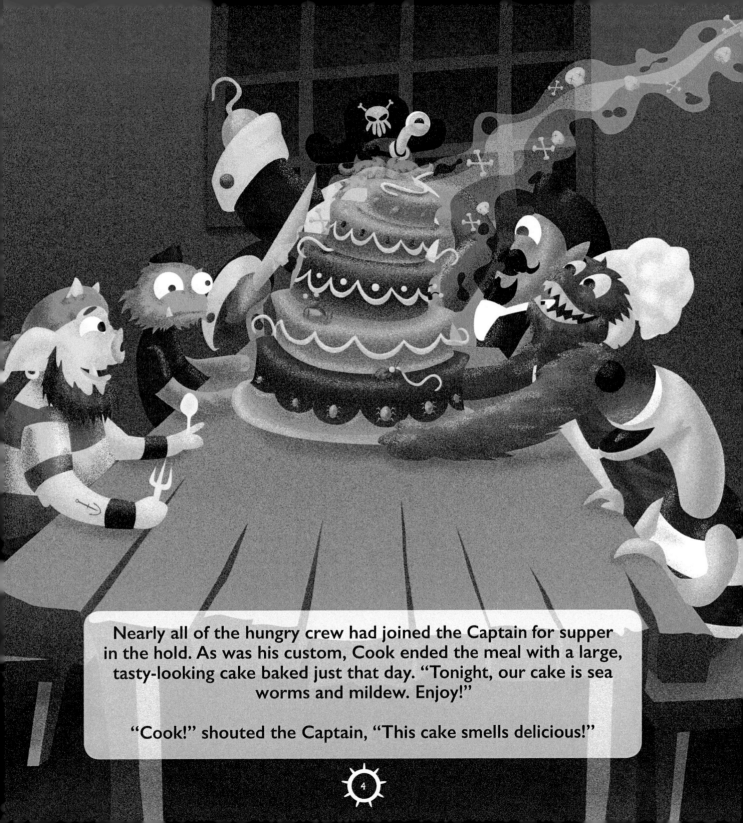

Nearly all of the hungry crew had joined the Captain for supper in the hold. As was his custom, Cook ended the meal with a large, tasty-looking cake baked just that day. "Tonight, our cake is sea worms and mildew. Enjoy!"

"Cook!" shouted the Captain, "This cake smells delicious!"

It was a very fragrant cake. So strong was the smell of sea worms and mildew,
it floated above the deck where Lazy Bob slowly pushed a mop and up into
the crows nest where Crabby Abby had watch duty. The odor even drifted out
across the water where a large, unseen monster swam.

Suddenly, the quiet night was interrupted by Crabby Abby's screams. A huge monster with glowing yellow eyes had appeared from the darkness! Roaring, it took hold of the ship and shook it about.

Inside the ship, Captain Dan and the crew found themselves tossed from one end of the cabin to the other for several long moments before a deafening CRACK filled the air. Then as suddenly as it began, the shaking stopped. The cake-covered crew could only wait for daylight to see what that cracking noise meant.

The next morning, the crew set to work repairing the damage on the Grumbling Grog under the watchful eye of Itchy Bill. Crabby Abby told the story of the angry Kraken over and over to any who would listen. Though a giant squid monster seemed a bit silly, not even Grouchy Tom could argue that something large had attacked the ship.

From that first night, the Grumbling Grog was never quite free of the vengeful squid. Weeks might pass with nary a sight, but eventually, the angry kraken would roar out of the blue depths and attack!

For nearly a year, the beast continued its determined assault.
No matter where the Grumbling Grog sailed, the kraken followed.

With no idea when the next attack would come, the crew began to get jumpy and nervous.

Crabby Abby, who was most partial to paydays, complained loudly, "That squid thing attacks only when we are chasing a ship or stealing treasure!"

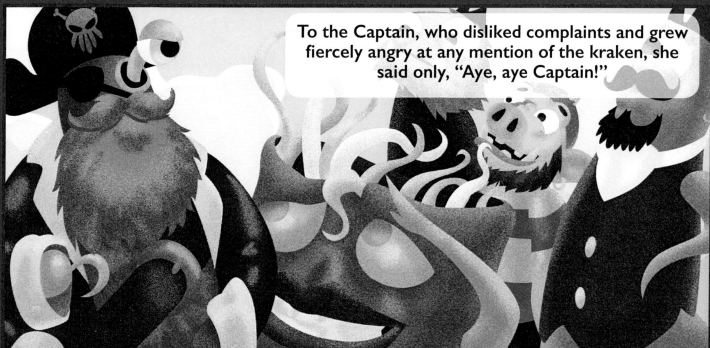

To the Captain, who disliked complaints and grew fiercely angry at any mention of the kraken, she said only, "Aye, aye Captain!"

But the crew noticed that Crabby Abby was not wrong.
The kraken seemed to attack just as ships surrendered.

Often, heavy ships full of delightful treasure got away while the Grumbling Grog was forced to fight a frightful kraken for no pay.

All work and no pay took a heavy toll on the pirate crew. Shifty, the ship's lookout, began to see glinting tentacles day and night. Sometimes, he failed to spot ships that should have been easy prey. Other times, he'd spot phantom islands that were not on any map.

Finally, First Mate Itchy Bill was forced to give Shifty a different job.

Shifty was not the only pirate to feel the effects of the kraken's sneak attacks. Cook began to regularly burn dinner. One particularly bad day, he forgot to bake the Captain's cake!

All over the ship, the crew of the Grumbling Grog made silly mistakes and grew slack in their chores.

Itchy Bill tried to explain how much "stress" the crew was under to Captain Dan, but the Captain was not in the mood to listen. "Assemble the crew and we'll see how much "stress" they be under!"

"Argh!" He shouted. "Ye lazy louts will be the end of the me!"
Pacing angrily across the deck, he continued, "What kind of
pirate crew is afraid of a fish?"

More angry than the crew had ever seen him, Captain Dan kept yelling. "I can't be the fiercest pirate captain to ever sail if me crew is weak-kneed over some stray guppy!"

With that, he ripped off his hat and threw it into the sea.

The crew stood hushed and sorry as Captain Dan continued to rant and pace. The Captain was very good at name calling, but this rant was one of his very, very best. So completely angry was he, and so fearful were the crew, that no one said a word when a tentacle slipped slowly over the side of the Grumbling Grog.

For a long moment no one spoke or breathed.

Itchy Bill broke the silence with a call to arms. "To Captain Dan!"

The whole crew peered anxiously into the waves slapping against the side of the Grumbling Grog, but there was no sign of Captain Dan. No stray bubbles or floating debris marked the spot where he'd disappeared.

26

"Oh no, oh no!" Cried Grouchy Tom. Cook sobbed loudly and blubbered something about worms and cake.

Tears forgotten, the whole crew rushed over.

It is whispered (for no one ever yells for fear of who might hear), that Captain Dan, the most feared pirate to ever sail the eleven seas has made a pet of an awesome sea monster.

"Never, ever run from Captain Dan," whisper old sailors. "For if he tires of chasing you, he might send out his fearsome pet..."

"Better the pirate you know than the kraken you don't."

Pin-up Gallery

BANANA SLUGS

SPENCER BRINKERHOF III

Made in the USA
San Bernardino, CA
09 July 2016